FANGS

VAMPIRE SPY

CODENAME: THE TICKLER

TOMMY DONBAVAND

WALKER BOOKS

First published 2013 by Walker Books Ltd
87 Vauxhall Walk, London SE11 5HJ

10 9 8 7 6 5 4 3 2 1

Text © 2013 Tommy Donbavand
Illustrations © 2013 Cartoon Saloon Ltd

This book has been typeset in Helvetica and Journal

Printed and bound in Great Britain
by Clays Ltd, St Ives plc

British Library Cataloguing in Publication Data:
a catalogue record for this book is available from
the British Library

ISBN 978-1-4063-3159-2

www.walker.co.uk

www.fangsvampirespy.co.uk

For Sammy,
who helps me to catch wild tickles!

MPI Personnel

Agent Fangs Enigma
World's greatest vampire spy

Agent Puppy Brown
Wily werewolf and Fangs's super sidekick

Phlem
Head of MP1

Miss Bile
Phlem's personal
secretary

**Professor
Hubert Cubit,
aka Cube**
Head of MP1's
technical division

A truck bearing the logo of the Addo National Park drove through a residential suburb of Port Elizabeth. As it passed the gates of a primary school, excited children clung to the railings, delighted to see that the lorry's cargo was a large grey elephant. The elephant trumpeted to a chorus of cheers from the playground.

Behind the wheel of the truck, Special Agent Fangs Enigma – the world's greatest vampire spy – arched an eyebrow. "Sound effects, too," he said to the young werewolf sitting in the passenger seat next to him. "Nice touch."

Fellow agent, and werewolf, Puppy Brown

smiled. "I thought you'd like it."

"Any sign of Snores yet?" Fangs asked.

Puppy studied the motor-vehicle-recognition software on her laptop and shook her head. "Nothing yet, but it shouldn't be long. This is the quickest route to the airport."

"And he'll definitely have the package with him?"

"He isn't likely to trust anyone else with it. According to a tip-off I got yesterday, he's asking for two hundred thousand dollars for it."

"Not a bad day's work," said Fangs. "Do we know what the package is yet?"

Puppy shrugged. "No idea. Only that he stole it from a government laboratory late last night. It seems us following him for so long has finally paid off. We have to stop him before he tries to leave the country and—"

An alert sounded on Puppy's computer.

"That's him," Puppy said, glancing at the screen. "Three cars ahead."

Fangs tapped his sunglasses to activate the

zoom function in the camera embedded in the lenses and scanned the traffic in front of them. "The yellow Mini with the tinted windows?"

"Those aren't tinted windows," said Puppy. "That's Snores!"

What Fangs had mistaken for a silver coating on the car's windows was, in fact, the skin of a huge grey ogre squeezed inside the tiny vehicle. He had rolled the windows down to allow his elbows to stick out as he steered. Suddenly, his head popped up through the sunroof. Turning, he looked straight at them, his trademark metal nose glinting in the sunlight. Then he slammed a foot down on the accelerator and the Mini roared away, tyres screeching.

Puppy loaded a live satellite view of the local area onto her laptop. "He's heading for the N2 highway," she said.

"We'll have to stop him before he gets there. If he makes it into heavy traffic, a Mini will have the advantage." Fangs accelerated, pushing the needle of the speedometer to 70 … 80 … then 90 miles per hour. The elephant's trunk swung wildly from side to side at the back of the truck.

Puppy opened a second window on her laptop and linked to the video feed from the camera in Fangs's sunglasses. "What's he doing?"

Snores had stuck one of his thick arms out of the car window and was dropping something floppy and yellow onto the road in front of them.

Fangs just had time to shout "Banana skin!" before their right front tyre clipped the peel. The skin exploded on impact, sending the truck spinning off the road and into a nearby tree. Thanks to the reinforced steel armour of the vehicle, both Fangs and Puppy were safe, but the engine was a charred mess of molten metal, flames still flickering across what remained of the bonnet. The lorry was a write-off.

"I think I may have concussion," said Fangs, rubbing his forehead. "I could have sworn that banana peel just exploded beneath us."

"It did!" Puppy growled. "And Snores will be on the highway in less than two minutes."

"Then it's time to take Jumbo for a spin," said Fangs, pulling the truck to a halt.

After leaping from the cab, Fangs and Puppy squeezed into the back of the lorry beside the fake elephant. The vampire wiggled one of the elephant's long tusks and a doorway in the creature's side slid open to reveal a tiny cockpit.

"It's a tight fit," muttered Fangs, climbing into the pilot's seat. He flicked on the engine as Puppy climbed in behind him. The elephant's ears rose and began to spin, slowly at first, but building up speed.

"*Ear* goes!" yelled Fangs over the noise of the engine. The animal lifted up into the air, its ears rotating at full speed and its trunk stretching straight out in front for balance. "Of all the gadgets Cube has invented, this '*ele*-copter' has got to be the most ridiculous."

Puppy was scanning the road below. "Got him!"

she said as she caught sight of the speeding yellow car. "He's about six hundred metres from entering the highway."

Fangs pushed the control stick forward, sending the *ele*-copter into a dive towards their target. "We'll stop him with the help of a little-known elephant martial art," he said.

"Martial art?" asked Puppy. "You mean like kung fu?"

"This one's called *dung* fu," Fangs quipped, and flipped a switch.

A massive, steaming pile of artificial poo dropped out of the elephant's bottom and landed with a *SPLAT!* on top of the Mini.

TOP SECRET
MP1 Mission File #2
Codename: The Tickler
Report by: Agent Puppy Brown

I pressed my paw against the security scanner outside the laboratory of Monster Protection, 1st Unit, aka MP1. The matrix of blue laser lights swept across the fur on my palm as the computer identified me. It's taken me quite a while to get used to having hairy hands – in fact, the whole werewolf thing has taken a bit of getting used to.

You've probably read stories about spooky things like vampires and werewolves. Guess what? They're not stories. It's all true! And ever since the supernatural equality laws were passed, creatures of all shapes and sizes have lived happily side by side. Well, almost everyone has. Just like in the human world, the supernatural one has its fair share of villains, and it's the job of MP1 to track them down and catch them – to protect the world from the very worst criminal *monster*minds. And I work for MP1.

You might also know that werewolves only transform once a month at full moon. But that's not how it works with me. Something went wrong during my first transformation and I ended up permanently stuck as a werewolf – claws, fur, fangs, the lot. Bad luck, huh?

There were a couple of werewolves in my school – but unless you happened to be with them at full moon, you never got to see them as wolves.

I'm the exact opposite. The full moon is the one night a month when I change back to a human girl. I became a joke to all my classmates.

My mum and dad tried to accept that their only daughter was now a slavering beast with teeth and claws, but life wasn't exactly pleasant any more. We stopped going for day trips to the seaside (no amount of shaving could make me look good in a swimming costume), and they always left me in the car when they went to the supermarket, with the window open for air. Life as a lycanthrope was making me miserable.

That all changed when I was recruited by MP1 and teamed up with Fangs Enigma – the world's greatest vampire spy (his words, not mine). Since then, life has been a whirlwind of weapons-training, computer-hacking and secret assignments.

"Access granted," said the voice of the security system. "Welcome, Agent Brown."

19

The silver doors to the lab swooshed open and I stepped inside. As ever, it was a hive of activity. Scientists tapped away on computers or assembled the latest high-tech gadgetry that had been invented specifically to help agents in the field.

I found what I was looking for in the engineering department at the back of the room. A mountain of dried elephant dung sat between the tool benches, and a technician was hacking at it with a vicious-looking pickaxe.

I glanced at the technician's name tag – "XD". None of the staff at MP1 headquarters use their real names, in case their identities are discovered and they become targets for ruthless bad guys.

"How's it going?" I asked.

XD lowered the axe and pulled off his safety goggles. "Not too well, I'm afraid, Agent Brown," he replied. "The fake dung was always designed to harden on impact, but we didn't realize it would be this difficult to cut through."

"So the Mini is still under all that?"

"With the suspect inside," XD confirmed. "We've got someone coming down with a chainsaw."

My werewolf ears twitched as they picked up a faint rasping sound, like the buzzing of angry bees. "I think I can hear it now," I said.

"That's not the saw." XD smiled. "That's coming from inside the car."

I pressed my ear to the hardened dung and listened. "Snores is asleep!" I exclaimed. "The noise would certainly explain how he got his nickname."

I left XD to his work and went in search of Fangs. He wasn't difficult to find.

"You fool, Cube! Everyone will think I've peed my pants."

I raced in the direction of the shout to see what had upset my boss.

Fangs was in the lab's administration office – and he was soaking wet. He looked as though he'd taken a shower fully dressed. He wrung water from his cape while glaring at Professor Hubert Cubit, the head of MP1's technical division.

Early on in life, the professor had realized that facts and information only ever came in square things. "Books, computers, filing cabinets – all square and all filled with knowledge," he told me during my first week of training. "Tennis balls,

potatoes and scoops of ice cream – all round
and hardly any knowledge in them at all."

Determined that he would also be stuffed
with information, the young
Hubert built a tight-
fitting wooden box to
wear like a hat at all times,
so changing the shape of his
head as it grew, from a useless
sphere to a fact-filled square. It is
for this reason that he is now known
within MP1 as "Cube", and right now his square
head was staring angrily at my boss.

"It was your own fault," Cube said. "You
shouldn't have taken the pen without permission."

"What's going on?" I asked.

"I'll tell you what's going on," said Fangs.
"I borrowed a pen from Captain Brainbox here."

"Without permission," Cube added.

I blinked. "And?"

"It's a new invention of mine," Cube explained. "A fountain pen – with a real fountain inside. Removing the lid unleashes a torrent of water."

"But Fangs is drenched," I said. "How can all that water have come from this normal-sized pen?"

"Technically, it didn't," said Cube. "The pen actually sprays out a chemical compound that draws water from the air around it. I invented it because I got so fed up with people taking my pen without asking – although you can borrow this one any time you like, Agent Enigma." He smiled.

"What else have you got for us today, professor?" I asked, trying to change the subject.

Cube's eyes lit up. "I'm so glad you asked, Agent Brown. What do you make of these?" He produced a bag of multicoloured balloons from his pocket.

"Don't tell me," said Fangs. "They explode in the face of whoever tries to inflate them."

"Don't be ridiculous," scoffed Cube. "No, these

balloons have helium atoms infused directly into the rubber. Try blowing one up..."

I chose a balloon and began to blow.

"No more need for bulky gas canisters," Cube enthused. "Instant, lighter-than-air balloons wherever you go. And they use hyper-helium, which is ten times more powerful than regular helium."

"That's very clever," I began – and then clamped a paw over my mouth. I sounded like a cartoon chipmunk. "What's happened?" I squeaked.

Cube smiled apologetically. "Unfortunately, I haven't yet found a way of stopping the helium from being breathed in by whoever inflates the balloon."

"You haven't found a way of inventing anything of any use at all," said Fangs.

"You may wish to take that back when you see my final offering," Cube said. He opened a drawer and handed over a plastic comb.

"Finally," said Fangs. "Something I can actually

use during assignments. Especially when I'm interrogating female suspects." He began to run the comb through his hair.

"No, Fangs!" cried Cube.

But he was too late. A thin, red laser beam shot from the end of the comb and hit a nearby table, burning a hole in its metal surface. Fangs jumped,

 accidentally aiming the laser down at his feet and melting the leather of his shoe.

"*AARGH!*" He pulled the ruined shoe off and then hopped around, clutching his toasted toes.

"You idiot, Agent Enigma," Cube snapped. "You've knocked the comb's focusing lens out of alignment."

"It wasn't my fault," Fangs retorted, examining the smouldering hole in his sock. "There's something wrong with that thing. It fired a laser at me!"

"It was supposed to!" said Cube, taking the comb from Fangs and carefully laying it on the table. "That's why it's called a *laser* comb."

"A what?"

"A laser comb," said Cube. "As soon as the coating on the plastic teeth makes contact with hair, a high-energy laser is fired from the handle. Thanks to your buffoonery, I'll have to take it apart and realign the lens."

"My buffoonery?" Fangs said. "You're the one who comes up with this useless stuff."

"I'd like to see you do any better."

"Ah," said Fangs with a smile. "That's exactly what I have done..." He reached into a pocket inside his cape and pulled out what looked like a TV remote control. Well, I'm guessing it had started out life as a TV remote. Now it had an aerial jammed into one end. And it looked as though someone had glued glitter all over it.

"What is that?" Cube asked.

"This is 'The Bloodhound'," said Fangs proudly. "I made it myself."

"I can see that," said Cube. "What does it do?"

"The Bloodhound can locate human blood at a range of up to five hundred metres," Fangs explained. "When it finds blood, it lights up and emits an alarm."

"Well, it doesn't appear to be working," Cube said. "I'm standing right in front of it and I'm full of human blood."

"That's because I've got it programmed to find blood that's already been donated and bottled," said Fangs. "I can't drink blood that's still inside someone. That would be vulgar."

I took the remote from Fangs and examined it. Some of the glitter came off on my fur. "So you've invented a way to find blood you can add to your glasses of milk?" I asked.

Fangs nodded. "I need never go without a blood milkshake again."

Cube choked back a contemptuous laugh. "It's the most ridiculous thing I've ever seen!"

"No, it isn't," Fangs said, taking the Bloodhound back from me. "It is a thing of beauty. And, unlike your amateurish gadgets, Cube, it works perfectly. Watch..." He stabbed at a button on the remote with one of his long nails.

Nothing happened. Well, almost nothing... I felt a sharp pain rocket through my teeth.

"Ow!" I cried, clamping a hand over my mouth.

"I can't hear any alarm, Agent Enigma," said Cube sarcastically.

"You just have to give it a moment to warm up," said Fangs. He pressed another of the glitter-coated buttons.

BOOM!

On the other side of the room, a laptop computer exploded.

"Hang on... I know one of these buttons works—"

"ARGH!"

A lab technician screamed as the mobile phone he was working on suddenly showered him with sparks.

Fangs continued to punch buttons to the accompaniment of cries of alarm from somewhere in the laboratory. Equipment was fusing out and blowing up all around us. And my teeth were really hurting.

Cube snatched the remote from Fangs's grasp. "Give that to me before you kill us all."

"It just needs a little fine tuning, that's all," protested Fangs. "Then it will be more use to us on our assignment than any of your pathetic creations."

"But we don't know what our mission is *yet*," I said. "We're still not sure what it is that Snores stole."

"I can tell you that," gargled a voice behind us. It was Phlem, the head of MP1, and he didn't sound happy. But then he rarely is.

Phelm is always covered from head to toe in dripping green ooze, and legend says that he is the only slime beast ever to have survived outside the gloopy waters of the fabled black lagoon.

"Follow me..." he said.

Fangs and I followed Phlem through the maze of corridors that make up MP1 Headquarters, careful to avoid slipping on the slimy footprints he left behind. I wasn't sure where he was taking us. Fangs had retrieved his remote control from Cube when we left the lab, and he was fiddling with it as we walked.

"This is a copy of what Snores stole in South Africa," Phlem said, opening his hand to reveal a small red tablet. It seemed to glow slightly, as though lit from within. "It's called a Will Pill. It overrides the self-control of anyone who swallows it and allows others to direct their actions. It is currently loaded with my voice, so if you swallow this Will Pill, you'll do everything I tell you to until the pill passes out the other end."

"That's amazing," I said.

Fangs pressed a button on the Bloodhound. There was a **CRACK!** as the two halves of the Will Pill split apart in Phlem's hand. "Oops."

"It appears I'll also be able to show you how it works, thanks to Agent Enigma," Phlem glugged. "This" – he gestured to a microscopic circuit board inside – "sends electrical impulses to the brain. They are linked to a pre-programmed voice pattern, mine at present, as I said. I had Cube programme it in earlier. The model Snores has stolen is far more

33

advanced, however, and can have an unlimited number of command voices installed."

"What's it for?" asked Fangs.

"The pill was designed jointly by the British and South African governments," Phlem explained. "We plan to use it to 'encourage' foreign agents to work on our behalf, albeit temporarily and against their wishes."

"If something like this should fall into the wrong hands, sir..."

"Exactly, Agent Brown," said Phlem. "That's why we had you apprehend Snores before he could sell the Will Pill on. We want to know who's prepared to buy this technology and what they plan to do with it."

"You think he stole the pill to order?" I asked.

"That's our guess," said Phlem, "although this is a top-secret project. How anyone outside MP1 even knows of its existence is a mystery."

"Can't we just feed this pill to Snores and order

him to tell us who he stole it for?" I asked.

"Unfortunately, Agent Brown, while the Will Pill's toughened shell allows it to pass unharmed through a human's digestive system, the acids bubbling away inside an ogre's stomach are simply too vicious. We'd be waving goodbye to thousands of pounds' worth of delicate equipment."

"I can see how that would be *hard to stomach*," quipped Fangs, tucking his remote control away. "As is the entire concept. There's no pill in the world that could make me do something I didn't want to."

"I suspected that might be your reaction, Agent Enigma," said Phlem, snapping the two halves of the pill back together, "which is why I'm willing to provide a practical demonstration – at a considerable cost to the lab, I might add."

We had stopped in front of a steel door at the end of the corridor and Phlem swiped his security pass against the sensor beside it. We stepped out of Headquarters onto a busy street.

Businessmen clutched briefcases as they strode by, a lollipop lady showed school children across a zebra crossing and customers milled in and out of a nearby bank. Dotted among the humans were witches, skeletons, gnomes and other supernatural characters. People were so used to seeing creatures like us nowadays, that the sight of a vampire, werewolf and a slime beast chatting together hardly raised an eyebrow.

Phlem produced a packet of jelly beans from his pocket and dropped the Will Pill on top of the sweets. Then he approached the lollipop lady.

"Morning, Janice," he said amiably, eating a couple of the sweets himself. "Busy day?"

"Busy as ever, ducky," the lollipop lady replied. "And there's a bit of a chill in the air, too."

"There certainly is," said Phlem. "You make sure you stay wrapped up." Then he held the bag of sweets out. "Jelly bean?"

"Ooh, don't mind if I do," said Janice, dipping

her hand into the bag. I could tell from the way
Phlem was holding it that he was making sure
she would choose the Will Pill. I caught sight
of a flash of red as she popped the pill into her
mouth. "Do you know, even in winter some of
the kids—"

The lollipop lady froze and the pupils of her
eyes grew wide, as though someone had flicked an
"off" switch in her brain.

"Janice," said Phlem calmly, "I want you to go into the bank over there and steal a thousand pounds."

Without so much as a blink, Janice turned and strode into the bank. We followed her inside. She walked straight up to the nearest cashier.

"This is a robbery!" she screeched, whipping off her fluorescent yellow cap and pushing it through the gap beneath the cashier's window. "Put one thousand pounds in that hat or else."

Instantly, alarm bells began to ring and metal shutters slammed down, protecting the cashiers and – more importantly – their money.

"That's unbelievable," I said.

Fangs, however, remained unconvinced.

"Nothing but an illusion," he said. "I'll put a stop to it."

"You can't, Agent Enigma," bubbled Phlem. "The Will Pill is tuned to my voice pattern alone."

38

"Then stand back and watch *my* voice patterns at work," said Fangs. "I think you'll find them more effective than any pill..."

He took one of Janice's hands and spun her round, catching her in his arms. "Why don't you leave this life of crime behind and join me for some good food, excellent wine and burning romance?"

Janice gazed up into my boss's eyes for a moment, then raised her metal lollipop in the air and brought it down onto his head with a

CLANG!

"I stand corrected," groaned Fangs as he staggered back to join us. "The Will Pill *does* work, after all."

"And Snores is due to sell one this evening," said Phlem. "We'll have someone making the drop in his place, and you two will be waiting to pounce once the deal is done."

Police sirens could be heard approaching in
the distance.

"Er ... will Janice be all right, sir?" I asked.

Phlem nodded. "I'll get a clean-up team down
here to sort everything out. They'll flush the Will
Pill out of her system and she'll be back at her
zebra crossing by the time school ends."

Phlem was interrupted by a voice coming from
my mouth. Just like Fangs, my front teeth had
been equipped with state-of-the-art blue-tooth
communication technology, and technician XD
was using it to contact me. "We're almost through
to the Mini, Miss Brown," he said.

Back in the lab, the technicians were cutting away
the last chunk of fake elephant dung. The sound
of snoring was louder than ever now and clearly
audible over the rasp of the chainsaw.

Nearby, Cube was repairing the laser comb
on a workbench. "I've almost fixed it," he shouted

over the noise. "No thanks to Fangs Enigma, of course."

Before Fangs could answer, the door to the lab swished open and ... Cube stepped into the room. "How's it going with the comb?" he called.

My eyes flicked from one Cube to the other. "How? Wh-what?" I stuttered.

Suddenly, the Cube at the workbench began to change. His skin rippled, like the surface of a pond after you've tossed in a pebble. His face, hair and clothes all rearranged themselves until there was a beautiful young woman with bobbed blonde hair standing before us.

"Holly!" exclaimed Fangs.

"Holly?" I said. "You're Agent Holly Delta?"

"The fastest shapeshifter in the business." Holly smiled and shook my hand. She turned to my boss. "Good to see you again, Fangs. It's been a while."

Fangs whipped off his sunglasses and smoothed back his hair.

41

He was engaging in what I've come to call his "chat-up mode".

"Too long," he crooned. "What say we catch up over dinner this evening?"

Holly adjusted Fangs's shirt collar. "I have very expensive tastes, and I doubt you could afford to keep me in the manner to which I plan to become accustomed. But we will be together this evening. I'm taking Snores's place at the handover."

Fangs kissed the back of Holly's hand. "Until tonight, then."

I rolled my eyes as my boss slinked over to the other side of the lab. Chuckling, Holly turned back to carry on her work on the comb. She soldered wires into place on the tiny circuit board.

"Where did you learn to do that?" I asked.

"Which one?" said Holly. "Repair laser combs or deal with Fangs Enigma?"

I tried not to smile. "The comb thing."

42

"I started out as a lab technician," she said, firing the laser beam at a nearby target to test it was working. "Once they discovered I was a shapeshifter, though, they figured I was more useful to them out in the field."

Behind us, there was a

THUD!

and the two halves of elephant dung split open to reveal Snores and his yellow Mini. Snores was fast asleep. I hoped he'd stay like that while we searched him for the Will Pill. It would be easier that way.

"Stand back!" said Fangs, rolling up his sleeves. "I'm the senior agent here. I should be the one to retrieve the Will Pill. Now where is it?"

Technician XD ran a hand scanner over the car, and up and down Snores's body. The sensor began to beep as soon as it was held near the ogre's massive metal nose. "It's in there, sir," he said.

Fangs paused. "On second thoughts, I can't take all the credit for stopping Snores. And it would be good experience for Puppy to conduct the search..."

"Thanks a lot, boss," I said, stepping up to the sleeping ogre. This wasn't going to be pleasant.

I thrust my claw up Snores's right nostril. It was filled with gooey, crusty bogies and I hoped that I wouldn't have to search the other nostril. But then, I felt something that *wasn't* a bogey. I hooked the end of my nail around the solid lump and pulled it free.

There, in the centre of my hairy palm, covered in thick, green snot, was a red, glowing Will Pill.

Fangs set the autopilot to maintain current speed and altitude and left the cockpit of the jet to join Holly and me in the cabin, where he poured himself his favourite drink – a glass of milk with a tiny drop of human blood. Then he took the Bloodhound remote from his cape and pointed it at the glass. "Now," he muttered, "it has to work this time."

He hit a button.

SCREECH!

Alarms blared from the cockpit as the autopilot
was disabled, and the jet began to dive. I stood
up to fix it, but was forced back into my seat
as another sharp burst of toothache hit me.
Holly rolled her eyes at Fangs and hurried to
the controls to get us back on course. The plane
levelled out a few moments later.

Cube's team had found an encrypted message,
probably given to Snores by the buyer, in the glove
compartment of his car. It had taken a little decoding,
but MP1 now had the exact details of the drop:

**Parking Lot, East 12th Street,
New York. 10 p.m., Sunday 29
March. $200,000. Caramel Cole.**

"Do we know any more about this Caramel
Cole?" asked Fangs.

I fired up my laptop as Holly rejoined us.

46

"I've got a call from Cube coming in now. Maybe he can give us more details."

A second window opened up on my laptop screen, this time of a page from an Internet video-hosting site. The footage playing showed a ringmaster in a tatty, red suit and silver top hat. The man was in his early forties with greying hair and a potbelly that hung over his belt. He was standing in the middle of a circus ring as four white horses galloped in a circle around him.

"Caramel Cole is a small-time circus owner based in Connecticut," said Cube over the video. "He started out selling toffee apples – or 'candy apples', as Americans call them – at state fairs, hence the nickname 'Caramel Cole'. Eventually, he saved up enough money to buy a second-hand big top, and he took his own circus on the road.

hoping to be the next great showman, along the lines of P. T. Barnum. Unfortunately, shoddy acts and low audience numbers have meant that his show has remained somewhat second-rate."

"You can say that again," said Holly.

On screen, the horses were leaving the ring and a beautiful girl with jet-black hair dashed on. She was dressed in a sparkling bikini and was clutching a pair of long, lethal-looking swords.

"This is Wanda Howe," said Cube. "A young lady with a remarkable skill."

Wanda dropped to one knee, threw her head back and lowered the sharp tip of the sword into her open mouth. She swallowed it bit by bit until only the handle was visible.

"Just your type, Fangs," said Holly with a smile. "If she can swallow swords, she might just be able to *swallow* your chat-up lines without choking."

I closed the video screen to reveal Cube's angular head. "I still don't understand. Why

48

would a small-time circus owner like Caramel
Cole want to get his hands on a Will Pill?"

"I guess that's what you'll need to find out
tomorrow," said Cube.

Fangs pulled the unmarked MPI car up to the kerb opposite a large, well-maintained apartment building. "This is the place," he said.

I checked the latest message from HQ on my laptop. "Phlem says that to avoid suspicion we shouldn't agree to sell the pill for anything less than two hundred thousand dollars."

50

Holly whistled appreciatively from the back seat. "Two hundred thousand. Imagine what we could do with that much money."

Fangs turned to smile seductively at Holly. "We could run away together and sip exotic cocktails in a tropical paradise."

Holly closed her eyes and sighed. "Sounds wonderful, apart from the fact that you'd be there with me." She jumped out of the car. "Come on, time to get into position."

"So our little love game continues..." said Fangs, gazing after her.

We crossed the road and entered the car park beneath the apartment building. Once inside, blocked from view by a large four-by-four, Holly closed her eyes and gradually her skin grew thicker and turned grey. Her teeth became dirty stumps, and her nose took on the dull glint of rusting metal. She opened her eyes, which were now flooded with blood-red veins – and the illusion was complete.

"Incredible," I whispered, peering up at what was now an identical copy of Snores. "His own mum would never know the difference."

"Have you got the Will Pill?" Fangs asked.

Holly opened her fist to reveal the tiny, glowing tablet. It looked smaller than ever, nestled in her giant, grey palm.

"Keep it safe," said Fangs. "Or you could just swallow it now, and I'll tell you where to meet me for dinner."

"Only if I can come looking like this," said Holly, her voice now low and gruff.

"Maybe we'd better stick to the plan for the time being," Fangs said.

Holly gave me a sly wink and ambled off, just as a vehicle turned off the road and entered the car park.

"Looks like we're on," said Fangs, stepping into the shadows and drawing his cloak around him.

A tiny, bubble-shaped car, painted with multicoloured flowers, passed between the spots where Fangs and I were hiding and drove into the darkness of the car park. Its engine made a comical *CHUCK-AH, CHUCK-AH, CHUCK-AH!* sound, punctuated by the occasional *AWOO-GAH!* from the car's horn.

I strapped on my night-vision goggles. The shadows melted away, revealing that the car had pulled up next to Holly A man with grey hair and a potbelly climbed out. I tapped my tooth to open up a line of communication with Fangs. "It's him," I hissed. "Caramel Cole."

"Has he got any muscle with him?" Fangs asked.

"It doesn't look like it. No one else could fit inside that car." I paused, blinking as a second figure emerged from the tiny vehicle – and then a third. "I think my night-vision goggles might be faulty," I hissed. "Cole's henchmen look distorted."

"Distorted?"

"They've both got huge, floppy feet and round noses, and they're grinning like someone's painted their smiles in place." I zoomed in for a better look. "Wait! Their smiles *are* painted in place. They're clowns!"

"*Funny way* to do business," quipped Fangs. "Has Cole got the money?"

I watched as Holly held out her hand to reveal the tiny Will Pill. Caramel Cole nodded to one of the clowns, who took a thick envelope from under his hat.

"This is it," I said. "He's handing over the—"

BANG!

There was a noise like the crack of a whip and a blinding flash of light. My night-vision goggles flared white and I pulled them off, blinking.

"That sounded like a gunshot!" I cried. "Can you see Holly? All I can see are swirling green shapes."

Before Fangs could reply, there was the sound of doors slamming and an engine starting.

"Something's gone wrong!" I yelled.

As the car raced towards us, Fangs leapt out of his hiding place. He landed with a *THUD!* on the roof of the car and stretched himself over the windscreen, grabbing onto the wipers to avoid sliding off. The car swerved first left, then right as the driver tried to dislodge him – but Fangs clung on tight. Then one of the clowns leaned out of the window and hurled a custard pie.

It hit Fangs full in the face, and he was thrown from the car. He crashed to the ground, rolling over and over until he collided with a concrete pillar.

Tyres screeching, the car swung up the car-park ramp and out of the exit. Not slowing down for a second, it smashed through the barrier and disappeared onto the street outside, sounding its horn.

AWOO-GAH!

"Fangs!" I yelled.

"I'm fine," my boss said, wiping his face. "Although I'd be better if it was the bad guys in *custard-y* instead of me. Go and check on Holly!"

I ran as fast as I could down the slope to the spot at the back of the car park where the deal had been taking place.

"Holly!" I shouted, my heart thumping. "Are you OK?"

There was no reply.

I looked around, but I was still half-blinded from the flash of light and it was very dark beneath the apartment building. I pulled a flare from my utility belt and tore off its top. The entire car park was lit up by a harsh, white light.

Agent Holly Delta was gone.

I took my seat beside Fangs on the bench and handed him a toffee apple. "Sorry," I said. "This was all they had. I guess Caramel Cole really likes these things."

Fangs took one look at the toffee apple and turned up his nose. "Yuck! I'd rather eat the bench. I bet it *wooden* taste as bad!"

The terrible food and Fangs's awful jokes weren't the only reasons I wasn't relishing our trip to the circus, but this place was the only lead we had. MPI staff had sealed off the car park in New York and scoured every inch of it, looking for clues – but they'd found nothing. The Will Pill, it seemed, had disappeared, along with Holly.

The only good news was that the tests for gunshot residue had come back negative. That meant the bang hadn't been made by a gun, so the chances were, Holly was still alive, and the noise had been a diversion tactic while they grabbed her and the pill.

I looked around the big top. My parents had taken me to the circus in my pre-werewolf days, and I recalled the glamour and the glitz. This place couldn't have been more different.

The tent was faded and torn, and a cold wind blew through the holes in the canvas. The handful of audience members sat shivering in their coats.

In the ring below us, aged horses wheezed as bored-looking girls in leotards danced next to them.

The acts didn't get any better. Over the next hour we sat through a juggler who kept dropping his clubs, a trapeze artist whose weight threatened to bring the entire tent down around us with each swing, and a fire-eater who set his own hair ablaze and then ran away screaming.

The only act that interested Fangs in the slightest was Wanda Howe, the sword-swallower. Despite her tatty costume, Wanda was stunning. Long, dark hair tumbled over her shoulders, and her pale skin shimmered under the spotlight. White wings fluttered out from her shoulder blades. (She was a fairy!) The audience held their breath as she threw her head back and plunged a silver sabre down her throat.

"Impressive," said Fangs, "but I bet even she couldn't eat one of Cole's rotten toffee apples."

Finally, as the lights dimmed, Caramel Cole himself appeared in the ring. "Now, ladies and gentlemen – the highlight of tonight's show... Bring on the Cannon of Doom!"

Cole's two henchmen clowns pushed an enormous cannon into the ring.

"You may think that being fired from a cannon is dangerous enough," Caramel Cole continued, "but what if I were to tell you that our human cannonball is to land in *here?*"

The trapeze artist and juggler both shouted *"Oooooh!"* and pulled the cover off a large cage. Inside was a scrawny tiger.

One by one, the audience members began to sit up and pay attention. This was starting to get interesting.

The ringmaster beamed. "And what if we added some bees?"

"Whooooooh!" exclaimed the fire-eater as he opened a box, releasing hundreds of bees into the air. Some of the audience members shrieked in alarm at the sight of the buzzing swarm.

"But that's not all!" announced the ringmaster. "What if we covered our human cannonball in pieces of raw meat for the tiger to enjoy and honey to please these bees?"

Two showgirls, each carrying a bucket, then stepped up to the cannon and took turns pouring sticky honey and lumps of meat into the barrel.

A hush, punctuated only by the buzzing of the bees and the growls of the tiger, fell over the crowd in the big top.

"But who would dare undertake such a dangerous task?" asked Cole. "One of us? Or one of you?"

The crowd gasped. Surely no one from the audience would be crazy enough to do this...

Fangs began to laugh. *"Hee-hee-hee!"*

Caramel Cole looked right at him. "Do we have a volunteer?"

Fangs's laugh became a chuckle ... *"Ho-ho-ho!"* ...became a guffaw ... *"Ha-ha-ha!"* ... then as quickly as he'd started laughing, he stopped.

"Fangs," I hissed. "What's the matter?"

Slowly my boss got to his feet and, in a calm, clear voice, said, "I will be the human cannonball."

The audience leapt to their feet, applauding.

I grabbed my boss's cape. "What are you doing?"

"I will be the human cannonball!" he repeated, trying to shake me off.

I scrambled to my feet. "Fangs," I begged. "Please stop this!" I pulled off his sunglasses and jumped back with fright. My boss's eyes were completely glazed over.

"I will be the human cannonball," he said again, pushing me out of the way.

"We have a volunteer," cried Cole.

63

The audience cheered as Fangs arrived in the ring. Wanda Howe helped him into the cannon. Once he was out of sight, the crowd fell silent. The ringmaster lit the fuse.

My stomach flipped with terror, and I clamped my paws over my eyes, peeping between my claws. This couldn't be happening!

The bees buzzed furiously.

The tiger roared hungrily.

I crossed my claws and screwed my eyes shut.

Then the cannon fired.

BOOM!

"Ow!" yelled Fangs as I used tweezers to pluck the twenty-fifth bee sting from his forehead. "Can't you be more careful?"

"You want *me* to be careful?" I cried. "I'm not the one who volunteered to be dipped in honey and raw meat and then fired through bees into a tiger's cage! That's the very *definition* of not being careful."

65

After the stunt, I'd dragged Fangs away from the circus – all hope of interrogating Caramel Cole lost for the day. Luckily, MP1 has houses available in every major town and city, so we had somewhere to stay and tend to Fangs's injuries.

"I need a drink," my boss groaned. "I don't suppose there's any blood in the kitchen?"

I shook my head. "There's milk, though."

"That's something," said Fangs, pulling his glittery remote control from inside his cloak. "I can find the blood myself..."

"Oh no you don't," I said, taking the Bloodhound from him and putting it out of his reach. "I need my laptop in one piece, thank you. And I could do without the toothache. Now what can you remember about the cannon stunt?"

"I've told you," Fangs insisted, lying back on the settee and rubbing ointment into the stings on his arms. "I don't remember any of it. I felt something tickle me and then everything went black."

"Maybe *you* don't remember," I said, opening my laptop. "But plenty of other people do. They're already uploading video clips of the stunt to the Internet."

I turned the laptop round to show him, but he covered his face with his cloak and groaned. "We don't have to watch it, do we?"

"If we want to work out what happened to you, we do," I said. "You went from being bored to stupid stuntman in less than a minute – and I need to know why."

"OK." Fangs sat up as I clicked "Play".

Caramel Cole's face filled the screen. "...Or one of you?" he cried. Then the camera picked up the sound of laughter and focused on Fangs, who was jiggling around and chuckling like a hyena.

"This bit I do remember," he said. "I thought it was you tickling me."

I glanced at my razor-sharp claws. If I'd been tickling my boss, I'd have scratched him to pieces.

"I will be the human cannonball," announced the Fangs on screen for the third time.

"Do you remember saying that?" I asked.

The real Fangs shook his head. "What's wrong with my voice? It sounds like I'm half asleep."

We watched Fangs walk into the ring and climb into the cannon with a little help from Wanda Howe. A second later, he was shot, screaming, through a thick cloud of bees and into the tiger's compound. Luckily, he landed on top of the tiger, temporarily stunning it and so giving himself enough time to scramble out of the cage.

"I remember that bit." My boss shuddered.

"From before or after you started crying?"

"I wasn't crying!" Fangs snapped. "Some of

the honey had got into my eyes, and they were watering!"

"So that's the only thing you remember after you started laughing for no reason?"

"It wasn't for no reason. Someone was tickling me."

"Someone, or something."

"Something?"

I scrolled back to the beginning of the video. "Look," I said, pointing at the screen, "There's no one sitting near enough to reach you."

"Well, something was tickling me."

"I'm not saying it wasn't, but why can't we see it?"

I loaded the footage into the MP1 video-scanning software on my laptop. It allowed me to run the film in slow motion and strip away any extra elements. Then I played the clip again. Fangs was just beginning to giggle when I saw it.

"There!" I cried, freezing the image. "That's what was tickling you."

On the screen, hovering beside Fangs, was a creature about the same size as a book. It was wearing a green dress and cap, and tiny green shoes that curled up at the toes.

"It's a pixie," I exclaimed.

"It can't be," said Fangs. "She's got..." He paused to count. "Eight arms!"

"That would explain why she was so good at tickling you. Do you think it's possible she tickled you into a trance?"

"A trance?"

"A state of hypnosis, during which she was able to tell you what to do."

"That's ridiculous!" scoffed Fangs. "I wouldn't do something dangerous, just because some mutated pixie told me to."

"Unless she was using the Will Pill somehow," I suggested. "Could it have been hidden inside your toffee apple?"

Fangs shook his head. "I didn't eat it, remember?"

"There's more to this than meets the eye."

"And we're going to get to the bottom of it," said Fangs. "Puppy, we're running away to join the circus!"

As highly valued government agents, Fangs and I were able to ask MP1 for just about anything that would improve our chances of solving a case and bringing a villain to justice. Fast cars, jet planes, powerful computers – we'd used them all. But it was a bit of a surprise for Phlem when Fangs requested a battered old motor home.

72

The slime beast was peering at us from the screen of my laptop, which sat on a small, stained table inside the caravan. Fangs and I were wedged onto a tiny sofa opposite. "You will rendezvous with Caramel Cole's Circus when it arrives in Pittsburgh tomorrow morning," said Phlem. "We've been monitoring the show since it left Somerville. Its reputation is growing fast, and the circus is becoming more popular with every performance. Ticket sales are through the roof. Cole is taking on new acts all the time, so we don't think you'll have too much trouble convincing him to let you join the company."

"Is his eight-armed pixie still tickling audience members, sir?" I asked.

"She is, indeed, Agent Brown," Phlem replied. "Take a look at this Internet footage."

The video showed various members of the public engaging in unusual stunts while the crowd watched in amazement. A young woman wobbled precariously as she rode a unicycle through a ring of fire. A pensioner hopped on one leg while juggling three live scorpions. And a teenager dangled upside down from the trapeze by his toes. Each volunteer wore the same glassy, wide-eyed stare.

"How does the pixie gain control of them?" I asked. "She has to be using the Will Pill somehow."

"Precisely," said Phlem, his slimy face returning to the screen.

"We need answers quickly," he continued. "In the bread bin behind you, you'll find two pairs of contact lenses. While you're wearing them, you'll be able to see the pixie."

"Does Cube have any theories on how she manages to hide herself?" I asked.

"Nothing solid," Phlem replied. "We think it's a similar technology to that used in the old MP1 disguise chips. She's not invisible – merely shielded by a hologram that matches her surroundings exactly."

In the days before the supernatural equality laws were passed, humans would have panicked at the sight of a vampire or werewolf roaming the streets – even if they were on the side of law and order. So MP1 agents had tiny computer chips embedded under their skin that allowed orbiting satellites to beam down holographic disguises over them with pinpoint accuracy. To everyone around them, the MP1 agents looked like everyday humans.

"Talking of disguises," said Fangs. "What will our cover story be?"

"I'm emailing the files to you now," said Phlem. "Agent Brown, you will work backstage as Trudy Haslingden. You grew up in a circus family, where you specialized in caring for the animals and preparing them for their time in the ring. You started work at Chipperfield's Circus in the UK, but wanted to work abroad and so made your way to Moscow, where you joined the team of animal trainers at Circus Nikulin."

"Got it," I said. "Trudy Haslingden."

"My turn," said Fangs. "I was thinking something along the lines of a lion tamer, or maybe a strongman."

"Don't worry, Agent Enigma," Phlem went on. "We've chosen the perfect disguise for you. No one will ever suspect your true spy identity." It could have been my imagination, but for a second, it looked as though Phlem was smiling.

"Your back story, Agent Enigma," said Phlem, "is that you trained as a clown at the Jacques Lecoq Theatre School in Paris. You then moved to Russia to appear at the internationally renowned Moscow State Circus. That's where you and Trudy met and became friends. Now, you have twenty-four hours before Caramel Cole's Circus arrives in town, so I suggest you both spend that time studying your parts and getting used to your characters."

"We'll do that, sir," I said. "Won't we, boss?"

There was no reply.

"Boss?"

Fangs was staring into space. "A clown?"

"Do you have a problem with your role in this assignment, Agent Enigma?" Phlem demanded.

"No, sir," said Fangs. "Of course not, sir. You just haven't told me what my new name will be."

"Of course, Agent Enigma," said Phlem. "How remiss of me."

Once again, I was sure the briefest of smiles played across Phlem's rubbery lips.

"You will be known by your professional clown name," he said.

Fangs took a deep breath. "Which is?"

This time Phlem really did smile. "Wobblebottom."

I swept up yet another mound of stinking
elephant poo. The real stuff was a lot smellier than
the fake dung we'd used to trap Snores in his car.

I'd been mucking out various circus animals'
cages for the past few days. Caramel Cole had
believed our circus cover story and hired us on the
spot. Fangs had wanted to raid his caravan to look

for the Will Pill that night, but Phlem advised us to keep our heads down for a bit and get to know the rest of the travelling company. For me, that meant spending time with the various animal trainers and backstage crew, while Fangs hung out with the performers.

Thanks to our contact lenses, Fangs and I could see the pixie clearly at every performance. She spent most of the show perched high up on one of the trapeze platforms. As the moment for the audience stunt grew near, she would flap her wings, then swoop down and hover silently around the crowd, searching for a victim to tickle. Once she had chosen a target, all eight of her tiny arms would go to work, squeezing and poking at the person's sides. The result was always the same – the volunteer would giggle and squirm and then their eyes would glaze over and their pupils widen. At that point, the pixie would land on the person's shoulder and whisper in their ear, presumably telling them to volunteer for the good of the show. We still hadn't worked out how the Will Pill came into it.

I heard the gate behind me creak open and the telltale jingle of bells tied to clown shoes. "Hello, Wobblebottom!" I said cheerily, without looking round.

"You can drop the silly names," said Fangs grumpily. "We're alone."

My boss was dressed in his show costume: a large blue-and-green checked suit with a yellow shirt and bright pink tie. His face had been painted white, with black eyebrows and a huge red, smiling mouth drawn on. A large, red nose and multicoloured wig completed the outfit.

"Finished your rehearsals?" I asked, trying not to smile.

Fangs nodded. "Caramel Cole and his pixie pal are in the big top, planning this afternoon's stunt. This is our chance to search his caravan for clues."

We dodged through the crowds that were queuing for tickets for that afternoon's performance. Then we headed for the field behind the big top where the performers' caravans were parked.

"We won't have long," I said quietly as we made our way through the trailers. "I have to clean the bears out before the show."

It took me a second or two to realize that I was talking to myself. Where had Fangs got to? I retraced my steps and found him chatting to Wanda Howe, the circus's sword-swallowing fairy.

"At first I found your act a little *hard to swallow*," I heard him quip as I approached. "But it wasn't long before I got the *point*."

"Well, ain't you just the red-nosed cutie pie?" Wanda smiled.

Fangs took the compliment as an invitation to continue talking. "When you're on a diet, do you swallow pins and needles instead of swords?"

Wanda laughed. "Don't you have a rehearsal to get to?"

"Nope!" said Fangs. "All done. There are only so many ways you can get hit in the face with a custard pie, and I've pretty much nailed it."

"You're quite the smooth talker, ain't you?" said Wanda. "We could do with someone like you to explain our feelings to Mr Cole."

"Your feelings?" I asked.

"That's right," replied Wanda. "The other performers and I, well ... we're not happy with the way the public are getting all the attention around here. We haven't spent years fine-tuning our acts to be upstaged by someone from the audience who's willing to take part in some stupid stunt."

"Do you have any idea why audience members are volunteering for the show?" asked Fangs.

"No, I do not," said Wanda. "Mr Cole must be picking them out before they take their seats and bribing them, or something. It ain't right, I tell you. It makes me so sad to think that someone could get hurt in the ring."

We left Wanda and scurried away to check out Caramel Cole's caravan while we still had time.

"So," I said, once we were out of earshot, "it looks as though the rest of the cast aren't in on Cole's plans. We'll need to keep an eye on them. If they stand up to Cole before we find out how—"

"Shhh!" said Fangs.

We had arrived at Caramel Cole's caravan, and a row was going on inside. We ducked beneath the window to avoid being spotted.

"...I don't care how much you think you deserve. This money is going towards upgrading the show!"

"You said Cole was still at the big top," I hissed.

"He was," Fangs whispered back. "He must have come back while Wanda was busy chatting me up."

I was about to correct my boss on how the encounter had really gone when another voice rang out. It was a squeaky, high-pitched voice. The pixie's.

"Well, maybe we need to renegotiate our little agreement."

"You can't do that, Tickler," Caramel Cole roared.

Tickler. Fangs and I mouthed the name to each other at the same time.

I risked a glance through the caravan window.

Caramel Cole was sitting at a table that was piled high with money. The tiny pixie was stomping around the cash, glaring at him.

"I want my money *now!*" she screeched.

"But we're almost there," Cole said. "We've got confirmation that he's coming, and I need this money to make final improvements to the show."

"The only way to improve that show would be to scrap it and start again. It's about as exciting as one of your candy apples."

"Then maybe you should choose a better quality of volunteer."

The door to the caravan swung open suddenly and Caramel Cole stepped out. "What are you two doing here?" he demanded on seeing us. He closed the door behind him, so we couldn't see inside.

"We, er... We were coming to see you," said Fangs. "Isn't that right, Julie?"

"Trudy," I corrected him.

"Yes, of course. Trudy."

"Well?" said Cole. "I'm a busy man. What do you want?"

"We wanted to thank you for taking us on as part of the circus," I said. "We're very happy here."

"You'll be even happier tomorrow," said Caramel Cole. "I want you to gather the entire company together for a meeting in the big top in thirty minutes. I have some important news."

"Why?" Fangs asked. "What's happening?"

Caramel Cole smiled. "Chuck Starburger, the president of the United States, is coming to see tomorrow's show! And it is going to be televised!"

Fangs and I knew we had to act fast. We couldn't allow the president of the United States to be present while some crazy circus stunt was taking place. If something were to go wrong and the president got injured, Phlem would have us washing dishes in the MPl canteen for the rest of our lives.

I watched the first half of that evening's show

88

from the back of the tent – which wasn't easy as the big top was packed almost to bursting. The circus was more popular than ever.

Wanda Howe and the trapeze artists had already been on – and the clowns were up next. Caramel Cole introduced Wobblebottom, and Fangs rode into the ring on the smallest bicycle I had ever seen. He cycled faster and faster, ignoring a giant speed-limit sign. After he had completed a few laps, Lumpy and Grumpy, Coles's two henchmen from the New York car park, drove on in their clown car – which was now fitted out with flashing lights and a siren to look like a police vehicle. They chased Fangs around the ring, leaning out of the car windows to hurl custard pies at him.

The audience loved it! They jumped to their feet and applauded when Fangs was finally captured and arrested.

Balloon handcuffs were placed around his wrists and he was thrown into a fake police cell, where Cole and the clowns continued to pelt him with more pies and shower him with buckets of confetti.

Eventually, the cell was wheeled off-stage and the lights in the big top dimmed. Caramel Cole stepped into a spotlight to announce that it was time to choose a volunteer from the audience for the climax of the show. I glanced up to see the Tickler perched on the platform above him and knew this was my chance.

I left the big top and hurried to the caravan field. Once at Cole's caravan, I used my werewolf claws to pick the lock and then crept inside. After closing the curtains, I switched on my torch and began to search.

At first I didn't find much. The show's takings were sitting on the small table in the living area and there was nothing but dirty dishes and out-of-date ready meals in the kitchen – so I turned my attention to the bedroom. Except this wasn't a bedroom at all. Instead of a bed, there was a workbench that was so big I had to close the door behind me to get round it. Dozens of electrical components, including microchips, transistors and bits of wire littered the table. A nearby toolbox was filled with an assortment of screwdrivers, pliers and a soldering iron.

I spotted a piece of paper with a scribbled sketch of an electrical circuit, and studied it. I'm nowhere near as good as Cube when it comes to electronics, but I recognized the drawing as the circuit board inside the Will Pill – with a few modifications. The electric current had been reversed. But that meant...

I tapped one of my front teeth with my tongue to open up my communication link with Fangs. "Boss," I hissed. "Are you there?"

Fangs's voice buzzed from my other tooth.

"What have you got?" he said.

"I know how the pixie is controlling people,"
I said. "They've reversed the Will Pill."

"What?"

"Remember the effect the Will Pill had
on Janice the lollipop lady?" I said. "Phlem's
commands sent tiny electrical impulses to her
brain and made her act out his commands. Well,
the Tickler's doing it the other way round. *She
swallows the pill and *then* exerts her will on a
member of the audience."

"But why tickle them first?"

"I've no idea," I admitted. "But this should be
enough to get HQ involved. You call Phlem while
I collect as much evidence here as I—"

"Cole!" cried Fangs.

"What?"

"I've lost sight of Cole."

"He's not in the circus ring?"

Just then, I heard the main door to the caravan

open. Caramel Cole was back, and I was trapped in his secret workroom!

I flicked off my torch and stayed very still, hoping that Cole wouldn't come into the bedroom.

"Did you hear me, Puppy?" Fangs's voice rang out through my blue tooth. "I can't see Caramel Cole. He could be headed your way!"

I clamped a paw over my mouth to deaden Fangs's voice, but it was too late.

"Who's there?" cried Caramel Cole.

I quickly locked the door to the bedroom, but Caramel Cole must have heard it, because the door began to rattle. He was trying to open it from the other side!

"Tell me who's in there!" he shouted. "What are you doing in my caravan?"

I didn't know what to do. The lock on the door wouldn't last long and the bedroom window was far too small for me to squeeze out of. I'd have to be the Tickler to fit through there.

That was it!

"Open this door!" Caramel Cole roared.

I pulled one of Cube's helium balloons from a pouch in my utility belt and started to blow it up.

"Come out of there now, or I'll—"

"Or you'll what?" I squeaked, my voice high-pitched from the helium.

"Tickler? Is that you?"

94

"Of course it's me," I snapped, trying to
remember the way I'd heard the pixie speak that
afternoon. "Who else do you think would be in
here?"

"W-well, I thought it might be an intruder, or—"

"Don't be ridiculous," I squeaked. "Who would
want to break into a dump like this?"

"Wait a minute," said Cole. "I just left you in the
big top—"

"So?" I said, thinking quickly. "I can fly faster
than you can walk. Now, hadn't you better get
back there for the finale?"

"I'm going, I'm going," Caramel Cole groaned.

I heard the main door to the caravan slam shut.
I waited for a few seconds to make sure Cole really
was gone and then I pulled a camera from my utility
belt and took snaps of everything on the table. Cube
would be very interested in this. I'd never have
thought Caramel Cole was intelligent enough to alter
the Will Pill's circuitry in such a way.

Pictures taken, I unlocked the bedroom door and stepped back into the main living area of the caravan. I paused to wipe clean any surfaces I might have inadvertently touched and then opened the door to leave.

Waiting for me outside the caravan with folded arms was Caramel Cole. The Tickler was sat on his shoulder, grinning in delight. Behind them, Lumpy and Grumpy were holding Fangs, who had his hands bound by rope instead of balloons this time and a gag tied across his mouth.

"I admit that your impersonation of the Tickler was very convincing," said Cole. "You would have got away with it, too – if the real thing hadn't overheard your friend here chatting to you."

Fangs raised his eyebrows in a gesture of apology. I gave him a shrug in return. There was no way he could have known the tiny pixie was hiding near by.

Caramel Cole produced a bunch of keys from his pocket and nodded his head in the direction of the animal cages. "What say we take these two somewhere a little more uncomfortable for a chat?"

Caramel Cole unlocked one of the animal cages I'd swept out earlier that day. Lumpy and Grumpy untied our hands, removed our gags and then pushed us inside. Meanwhile, the Tickler darted about behind her friends, giggling at our fate.

"You won't get away with this, Cole," Fangs snarled as Caramel Cole locked the gate. "If the

Moscow State Circus finds out how you've been treating one of their favourite clowns—"

"Drop the act," spat Cole. "Not that you had much of an act to begin with. You're not circus folk at all. You're Special Agent Fangs Enigma and his sidekick, Puppy Brown."

I tapped my front tooth with my tongue. "This is an urgent message from Agent Brown to MP1 Headquarters. Do you copy? Repeat – do you copy?"

"I wouldn't waste your breath," said Caramel Cole. He pulled a glitter-coated remote control from his pocket and aimed it at me as he hit a button. I felt a sharp pain in my mouth as my blue-tooth communication system was deactivated.

"My Bloodhound," cried Fangs, adding "Ow!" as Cole directed the remote at him.

Caramel Cole slid the gadget back into his pocket. We had lost all contact with MP1 Headquarters.

"Where did you get that?" I asked.

"You're not the only ones who can search caravans, you know," said Cole. "I found this little beauty in your motor home this morning."

"But how could you know it would fuse our blue-tooth transmitters?"

"Because Fangs Enigma showed me himself," said Tickler.

I felt a cold chill run down my spine. "What?"

The pixie fluttered up to the bars of the cage. "Still want to go out with me, Fangs?" she squeaked. Then she began to grow. Her eight arms melted into just two limbs, and her body lengthened. The pixie wings withdrew into her shoulder blades as her feet touched the ground.

Finally, her hair became a blonde bob.

"Holly Delta!" I cried.

"The very same," said Holly with a smile.

"Thank goodness," said Fangs. He pointed to Caramel Cole. "Holly – arrest that man for stealing the Will Pill, then let us out of here."

"I don't think you get it, do you, sweetie?" said Holly. She wrapped an arm around Caramel Cole's waist. "He didn't steal the Will Pill. I did!"

"What?" Fangs cried.

"The underground car park in New York," I said. "You weren't kidnapped. It was a set-up."

"You catch on a lot quicker than your boss." Holly smiled.

"And the Will Pill..." I continued. "You used to work in Cube's lab, so you knew how to take the pill apart and set it running in reverse."

Holly nodded. "It was simple, really."

"But what about the tickling?" asked Fangs. "I still don't get the whole eight-arms bit."

"It's simple reflexology," said Holly. "I don't tickle my victims. I massage pressure points in their nervous systems to make them more susceptible to my instructions. The fact that it makes them laugh is just a pleasant side-effect."

"And you knew all along that we could see you doing it," I said.

"I recognized you both at the show in Somerville," said Holly. "I had hoped that our little stunt with the cannon might have killed you, Fangs, but no such luck. When you followed us here, we thought it best to wait until just the right moment to capture you."

"But, why?" demanded Fangs, gripping the

bars of the cage. "You were working for the government, with *me*, Fangs Enigma! That's got to be the greatest honour MP1 could bestow on you."

"MP1 used me," Holly said. "I loved working as a technician in Cube's lab – inventing gadgets, designing electronic devices and adapting field equipment. But once Phlem found out I could stretch my face and impersonate people, he took me away from all that. He wasn't interested in my technical skills – just in the way I looked."

"It's still important work," I pointed out. "Think of all the people you've helped over the past few years."

Holly glared at me. "People who never thank me – and never can because I'm a *secret* agent! We don't get the rewards or the adulation."

"Maybe not," said Fangs. "But you had the chance to go out for dinner with me. You still might, if you play your cards right..."

"I think Fangs means we have the satisfaction of a job well done," I said.

"Satisfaction?!" spat Holly. "How many fast cars can *satisfaction* buy me? How do I pay for a beach holiday with a 'job well done'? I don't want to help other people any more. I want to help me. I'm going to use my talents to make life better for *me*!"

"You know, you're seriously risking your chance of an evening of romance on the good ship Enigma." Fangs scowled. "In fact, I doubt I'll be allowed to date you at all once MPI imprison you."

"Imprison me?" asked Holly. "They'll have to catch me first."

"You may be able to transform into anyone you like," I said, "but this circus can't. We'll find you through Cole."

Holly threw back her head and laughed. "You think I want to stay part of this tinpot operation?"

"Do you mind?" Caramel Cole said. "I've built this circus up from nothing to become the biggest travelling show in the United States of America. Tomorrow, I perform for the president himself."

"All thanks to me," said Holly. "But I've had all the creepy clowns and sassy sword-swallowers I can take in one lifetime. Tomorrow, everything changes."

"I get it," said Fangs. "This time tomorrow, with the world's media watching, you'll reveal yourself as the real success behind Caramel Cole's Circus."

"Oh, Fangs," Holly said, stroking his cheek. "Your ambitions are so limited..."

"You're not going to get President Starburger to volunteer to be in the show, are you?" I asked, a bad feeling creeping over me.

"No," said Holly. "When I tickle President Starburger tomorrow, I will suggest he takes a very long holiday. A holiday from which he will never return. And then I shall take his place."

Her skin began to ripple and, within seconds, an identical copy of the American president was standing before us.

"You won't get away with it," I said. "You won't be able to resist filling your pockets from the White House coffers. As soon as the American people realize how corrupt you are, they'll vote you out."

"With the facilities at my disposal, I can have enough Will Pills made to ensure Congress changes the law to accept me as president for life. The American people won't get a look in." She sounded exactly like Chuck Starburger.

I turned to Caramel Cole. "And what do you get out of this?"

Cole smiled. "The 'president' will be so impressed by tomorrow's performance that he will make a donation of one billion dollars to my circus – direct from the US Treasury. My circus will become the best in the world!"

"You won't get away with this," Fangs snarled.

"Of course I will," said Holly. "Now, why not resign from MPl and rule the world at my side?"

"Never," said Fangs. "Truth and justice are the only mistresses for me."

Holly rolled her eyes. "I think I might throw up."

"You're forgetting something," I said. "You may be able to fool the rest of the world, but Fangs and I know the truth. You can't stop us from telling everyone what we know."

Holly changed back to her usual shape. "Yes, I can," she said. "I can kill you both."

"She's got a point," Fangs said to me. "Killing us would stop us from revealing what they're up to."

"No," said Caramel Cole. "I want them both alive. With you gone, Holly, I'll need something to replace your Will Pill volunteers. I can't creep up on people and tickle them myself. And what better than a nightly battle between an angry werewolf and a furious vampire?"

I shuddered beneath my fur. "What?"

"The world has gone soft," spat Cole. "Once upon a time, freaks like you would have been dragged from county fair to county fair, where people would pay to gaze at you in sheer horror. Now you're an acceptable addition to polite society. But ... if I were to capture a rogue werewolf and vampire who still held onto those old, violent ideals..."

"I won't do it," I said. "You can't make me fight Fangs. He's my best friend!"

"She's right," agreed Fangs. "You can't force us to do anything."

"Oh, but I can, and I will," said Caramel Cole. He turned to Holly. "Would you be so kind as to ensure these two keep our secrets to themselves?"

Holly grinned wickedly. Then her skin rippled again as she once more changed into the Tickler. She darted between the bars of the cage and flew straight for me, all eight sets of fingers twitching.

I fought the tickling feeling as she massaged my pressure points – but in the end, I couldn't help but giggle.

Then she began to whisper in my ear, and the world went black.

"Puppy ... PuPPY!"

I forced my eyes open as a blast of cold water
hit me in the face.

I looked around. I was in a cage surrounded by
chunks of raw meat. Fangs was a few metres away

in a cage of his own, and he was spraying me with water from Cube's fountain pen.

"OK, OK," I glugged as another jet hit me in the face. "I'm awake." I pulled myself to my feet. "How long have I been asleep?"

"You haven't been asleep," said Fangs. "You've been in a trance for hours and hours. We both have. I came round about fifteen minutes ago and I was back in my normal clothes." He clipped the lid back onto the fountain pen and tucked it into his pocket. "What did the Tickler whisper to you?"

I thought hard, but my mind remained blank. "I can't remember."

"Neither can I," Fangs admitted. "Let's get out of here."

I looked down at my waist – my utility belt was gone. I still felt woozy and I wanted to sit down, but the floor of my cage was covered in what appeared to be blood. Chunks of raw meat also littered the floor. I picked one up. "These are made of rubber," I said. "And this is stage blood. It's all fake."

"I think it's Cole's way of making you look like a violent werewolf," Fangs said. "I've got plastic bats in my cage." He was silent for a moment. Then he said, "You know I don't want to fight you?"

"I know," I said. "But with Tickler around, we may not have a choice. We have to get out of here."

"We will," Fangs assured me. "I just need to—"

He was interrupted by approaching voices.

"...And this, Mr President, is our newest attraction – the Fighting Freaks. I wanted you to be the first to see it."

The tent flap lifted and Caramel Cole stepped inside, dressed in a brand-new, sequined ringmaster's waistcoat and hat. He was followed by four men in dark suits and Chuck Starburger, the president of the United States. "Well, well ... what do we have here?" The president beamed.

I began to smile.

Caramel Cole had made a big mistake. The US president knew all about MP1 – there was even a branch of our organization in Washington D.C. He'd listen to me.

"Mr President," I began, "it's very important that you-oooOOOOOWWWLLL!" I hurled myself against the bars of my cage and roared angrily.

President Starburger stared at me in horror

I staggered back, shocked. I hadn't meant to do any of that. "I'm sorry," I croaked. "But I have to tell you-ooOOOOOWWWLLL!" Once again, I flung myself against my cage, this time pushing my paw between the bars and raking at the air with my claws.

What was happening to me?

"Fangs," I hissed. "You have to tell the president what's going on." But my boss was unable to help. He was hanging upside down in his cage, his cape wrapped around him like the wings of a bat.

President Starburger approached our cages cautiously.

"Now you ain't gonna tell me this here werewolf and vampire are going to fight each other, are you?" he asked Caramel Cole. "Surely those days are long gone."

"Not for these two, Mr President," said Cole. "We found them tearing each other apart in the Rocky Mountains a few weeks ago. They haven't integrated into society at all. Caging them was the kindest thing we could do."

"No!" I cried. "That's not true-oooOWWWLL!" I roared again and rattled the bars of my cage. I couldn't speak about the plan. Every time I tried I ended up howling.

The president burst out laughing. "Well, ain't that somethin'." He slapped Caramel Cole on the back. "You sure know how to put on a show, boy!"

"Speaking of which," said Cole, "the show is about to begin, so if you would like to follow me..." He led the president and his men out of the tent.

I slumped back against the cage. The Tickler must have used the power of the Will Pill to make us pass out and prevent us from telling anyone about their plans. I shuddered to think what would happen if and when she ordered us to attack each other.

As soon as the president and Cole had gone, Fangs slumped to the ground. "Thank goodness," he said. "The blood was starting to rush to my head, but I couldn't move at all. It must have been the Tickler's spell. I almost ended up with rosy cheeks."

"Let's get out of here," I said, bending to peer at the lock on my cage. I wasn't sure if I would be able to pick it with my claws.

"Just as soon as I've straightened myself up a little," said Fangs. "Wanda's out there somewhere." He pulled a plastic comb from his pocket and began to tidy his hair. As he did so, a red laser beam shone from the handle, just as it had done back in the lab.

Fangs squealed and jumped back in alarm.

"That's brilliant, boss," I cried.

Fangs looked from the comb to me and back again. "It is?"

"Of course. You're going to use Cube's laser comb to burn through the locks on our cages."

"Er ... yes," said Fangs. "That's exactly what I'm going to do. Well done for spotting it, Agent Brown. Now, stand back and cover your eyes..." Cautiously, he began to comb his hair again, this time aiming the laser directly at the lock on his cage. The metal hissed and spat as it melted away.

Two minutes later, as the lock from my cage fell to the floor, we heard the circus music begin to play.

"The show's started," said Fangs. "Come on."

We were dashing out of our tent and racing
for the big top when a horrible thought occurred
to me. "Boss," I said, grabbing Fangs's arm to stop
him. "The president and his men think we're wild
supernaturals, ready to tear each other's throats
out. I dread to think what they'll do if they suspect
we've escaped from our cages."

"Then we'll need a disguise." Fangs looked
around and spotted the caravan belonging to
Lumpy and Grumpy on the other side of the field.

The lock on the clowns' trailer was easy to pick
with my claws, and once inside, we found spare
bits of costume and plenty of make-up. Fangs
picked out a strongman's leotard and boots.

"This looks ridiculous," I said, peering at
myself in the mirror. No matter how much make-
up I used, I couldn't hide my fur. "I look like a
poodle."

"There's a ballerina's costume hanging up over
there," said Fangs, pulling on a pair of spotted

braces. "With the white face paint and the tutu, you'll look just like a performing puppy, Puppy."

As much as I wanted to argue, I knew we didn't have long. So, a few minutes later, the new strongman and Trudy, his canine sidekick, were charging across the grass towards the entrance of the big top.

The horses and their riders were just coming to the end of their act as we pushed our way through the backstage area and invaded the circus ring. The four dancing girls – now dressed in brilliant, white-feathered costumes – glanced nervously at us as we dashed onto the stage.

"What is the meaning of this?" Caramel Cole cried. He raced towards us, microphone in hand. He grabbed Fangs by his leotard. "How did you get out?" he demanded, his voice echoing through the sound system.

Fangs snatched the microphone from Cole's grip. "Ladies and gentlemen, my name is ... er

Rocky Thunder. I'm the circus strongman. And the president is in terrible danger."

The big top fell silent – and then President Starburger began to laugh.

Seeing that the president was enjoying himself, the tension in the crowd vanished and they began to laugh along with him, thinking that this must be a special performance that had been arranged for the president's visit.

I glanced up and saw the Tickler glaring at us, so I left Fangs to deal with Cole and ran for the ladder leading up to the trapeze. Climbing in a tutu wasn't the easiest thing I'd ever done, but I knew I had to keep moving. I looked down to see Caramel Cole trying to wrestle the microphone from Fangs's hands. The audience, still thinking this was part of the act, was howling with laughter.

I climbed onto the tiny platform, high above the ground, and faced the Tickler. "This is over, Holly," I said. "Give yourself up."

But before the tiny pixie could reply, Cole finally got control of the microphone. "Tickler, do it now!" he screeched.

I threw myself across the metal platform, hand outstretched, but the Tickler simply flapped her wings and rose into the air. "It's over, all right," she squeaked. "Over for *you!*"

Then she plunged into a dive – heading straight for President Starburger.

She landed on the president's shoulder and began to climb down his jacket to reach his waist. At first, I couldn't understand why his security team didn't pull her off – and then I remembered that only Caramel Cole, Fangs and I knew where she was. The bodyguards were completely oblivious to the fact that the president was under attack.

I looked down to see that Fangs was wrestling with Caramel Cole – the audience was cheering them on. They still thought this was part of the show.

Below me, the Tickler began to tickle Chuck Starburger's belly. *"Hee-hee-hee!"* cried the president. *"HO-HO-HO!"*

Even from this height, I could see that the president's expression was glazing over and his pupils were growing wide. He was under the spell of the Will Pill and would now do whatever the Tickler told him!

With Fangs still grappling with Caramel Cole, I knew it was up to me to save the president. I threw myself off the trapeze platform.

The Tickler was whispering into the president's ear when...

CRASH!

I landed on top of President Starburger and sent him tumbling to the ground, with the Tickler still clinging to his shoulder.

The crowd let out a scream. A flying poodle had just attacked the president live on national TV!

"Freeze!" one of the bodyguards said. "You're under arrest for assaulting the president of the United States."

"I'm an MPl agent," I cried. "And I've just saved his life."

The bodyguard held his position. "How?"

I pointed to the Tickler, who was still hanging onto the president's jacket. "I know you can't

see her," I explained, "but the presidooooooooo-
OOWWWWLLL!"

The bodyguard looked bemused. "What?"

"She's right there!" I cried. "On the president's
shoooOOOOWWWLL!"

It was no good! I was still under the Will Pill's
influence and couldn't tell anyone what was really
happening.

"Come on, Puppy." The pixie grinned. "Spit it
out." Then she went back to whispering
in President Starburger's ear.

"Fangs," I cried.
"The Bloodhound."

Fangs knocked Cole to the
ground with his fist. Then he
snatched the glittery remote from
the ringmaster's pocket and hurled it at me.

In one move, I caught the Bloodhound, aimed
it at the Tickler and stabbed a button. "Say hello to
the nice security people," I snarled.

Her disguise chip was instantly deactivated, and she shimmered into view. The president cried out in alarm and knocked the tiny creature from his shoulder while his security team quickly surrounded him.

"You're too late!" the Tickler spat. "I've already told the president to pack up and leave the White House as soon as possible. I'll have taken his place by nightfall."

"No, you won't," I said. "You're going to give yourself up."

The pixie laughed. "And what gives you that idea?"

I smiled. "You did..."

The Tickler's smug grin faltered. "Wh-what?"

"If Fangs's Bloodhound can disrupt my blue tooth and your disguise chip, then let's see what it does to the Will Pill." I pressed the remote control into the Tickler's stomach and activated the device.

"No!" she screamed. "You can't do that. It will reverse all my alterations. I'll be completely ... under ... its ... control... I'll have to obey everything *anyone* says."

The Tickler's eyes swam out of focus. It had worked!

"Now," I said, "I want you to show these nice bodyguards your true shape, and tell them exactly what you planned to do – after which you will undo everything you whispered to the president."

For the final time, the creature known as the Tickler flapped her wings and rose into the air. Then she began to grow and stretch as she transformed back into Agent Holly Delta. The president and his men stared in amazement, as did the circus audience and, I imagine, the millions of people watching at home.

"I have something to confess," she said. "I have been trying to depose the president of the United States with the help of Caramel Cole."

There was a yelp from the circus ring. I turned just in time to see Cole making a dash for the exit. Fangs was on his heels in a split second, and I quickly followed.

We chased Caramel Cole out of the big top and into the sunlight. He pushed his way through the crowd, knocking over food stalls and dragging stacks of prizes to the ground in an effort to stop us following him. Fangs and I leapt over a pile of

tumbled teddy bears and struggled to keep sight of Carl's sequined waistcoat.

Bernie Gobb, the fire-eater, stepped out from behind the carousel in front of Cole, forcing him to stop. "Mr Cole," he said. "We want to talk to you!"

"Not now," barked Caramel Cole, darting to his right – only to find someone else in his way.

"Yes, now," Cass Cade, the juggler, insisted.

Cole turned left, but his escape route was

blocked by Wanda Howe. "What's going on here, Cole?" the sword-swallower demanded. One of her silver stage sabres was levelled at his chest. "It's bad enough you putting the public at risk to line your own pockets, but attacking the president as well!"

Cole tried to fight his way through the circus acts closing in around him. "Get out of my way," he bellowed.

"Not until we get some answers," shouted one of the horse riders.

"That's right," cried Bullet Drop, the leader of the trapeze troupe.

Caramel Cole's eyes were wide with terror. Whenever he turned, he found himself faced with another angry performer. There was no way out! And then a hand clamped down hard on his shoulder. It was Fangs.

"We'll be able to answer your questions," my boss told the circus performers, "just as soon as we've put this guy away. Caramel Cole, you are under arrest for— ARGH!" He sank to the ground, groaning in pain.

Cole had snatched Wanda's sword and sunk it deep into Fangs's right thigh.

"Oh no," shouted Wanda. "You do not do that to such a sweet clown, or strongman – or whatever he is now – especially not with one of my own swords."

As one, the circus performers took a step towards Caramel Cole. He was surrounded. But he still had one route he could take ... up!

After leaping onto the spinning platform of the carousel, Cole began to climb the pole of one of the wooden horses. Leaving Fangs to be tended to by Wanda, I went after Cole.

Having reached the top of the pole, Caramel Cole pushed one of the wooden tiles in the decorated ceiling of the carousel aside and disappeared through the gap. I followed, to emerge on the roof of the twirling merry-go-round.

I fixed my gaze on Cole – or, more specifically, on the drops of Fangs's blood dripping from the blade of the sword he was still clutching. Not only would keeping my eyes on one fixed point stop me from getting dizzy as we spun round and round, but I wanted to keep his weapon in view at all times.

"Give yourself up, Cole!" I shouted, trying to make myself heard over the music of the carousel. "The show's over."

Caramel Cole grinned wickedly. "Haven't you heard?" he snarled. "The show's not over until the fat lady sings – or, in this case, until the werewolf dies!"

Cole aimed the tip of the sword at my chest and then lunged forward. I threw myself out of the way just in time, grabbing at the iron struts that held the wooden roof of the carousel in place. With a scream, Caramel Cole flew past me and tumbled over the edge.

I clung onto my handholds as the carousel finally slowed to a stop. Then I dragged myself to the edge of the roof and peered over. Caramel Cole had landed head-first in his brand-new candy apple machine.

Fangs, the wound on his leg bound by a strip of material from Wanda Howe's costume, hobbled over. He grabbed Cole's feet and pulled him out. The circus owner's head was encased in a huge ball of glistening red toffee. His wide eyes and grin were fixed in place for ever.

Fangs glanced up at me. "Now that's what I call coming to a *sticky* end."

CASE CLOSED

SIGNED: Agent Puppy Brown

"Who wants another hot dog?" President
Chuck Starburger, sleeves rolled up to the elbow,
plucked a sausage from the roaring barbecue and
dropped it into a bun.

Bernie Gobb, the fire-eater, who was dressed
in his stage costume of blue serge with red silk
flames, took the snack, slathered it with mustard
and then took a big bite. "Oww!" he yelped.
"That's hot!"

The entire circus was set up on the lawn of the
White House, although the cast and crew were
under strict orders to relax for the day and the big
top was only there to provide shade from the glaring

137

sun. The company had been invited as a way for the president to thank them for saving his career.

An elephant stomped its way across the grass. On its back was a young werewolf whom the circus family had met as animal trainer Trudy Haslingden, but now knew was really MP1 agent Puppy Brown. They had assured her that her secret was safe with them.

Puppy slid down from the elephant's back, and led the beast to a bale of hay in the cool shade of the big top. She patted its trunk, eyeing the queue for food at the barbecue.

As she approached the president, a security agent in a dark suit and sunglasses took her paw and led her gently to one side. "Excuse me, miss," he said politely. "You have a call." He handed Puppy a mobile phone.

"Hello?"

"Agent Brown!" gurgled the voice at the other end of the line. It was Phlem. "Where are you? I've been trying to contact you via your blue tooth."

Puppy ran her tongue over the deactivated fang protruding from her upper jaw. She could have asked the MP1 technicians here in Washington to repair her broken blue tooth, but she figured she deserved a break.

"We're, er ... we're experiencing some problems with our teeth at the moment, sir," she said. "But we're hoping to be back up again soon. Has Holly Delta arrived in London yet, sir?"

"She certainly has," Phlem bubbled, "and she's facing a long time behind bars. Very tightly spaced bars that she can't shapeshift or squeeze between to escape."

"Fangs and I were hoping that would be the case, sir."

"Speaking of Agent Enigma," Phlem slobbered, "is he all right? My contacts say he was injured in the course of bringing Caramel Cole to justice."

Puppy glanced across the White House lawn to the sunlounger where her boss was lying with his leg wrapped in bandages. The cut hadn't been too deep, but he'd need to stay off his feet for a while. Sitting beside him, Wanda Howe spun one of her stage sabres and plucked a rare steak from the president's barbecue. Fangs began to devour it as the sword-swallower gently stroked his hair. At the foot of the lounger, two of the circus's showgirls wafted a cool breeze over him with their costume feathers. Fangs spotted Puppy looking in his direction and raised his ice-cold glass of milk and human blood in a toast to their success.

The werewolf smiled. "I think he might just pull through, sir."

ABOUT THE AUTHOR

TOMMY DONBAVAND was born and brought up in
Liverpool and has worked at numerous careers
that have included clown, actor, theatre producer,
children's entertainer, drama teacher, storyteller
and writer. He is the author of the popular thirteen-
book series Scream Street. His other books include
Zombie!; *Wolf*; *Uniform*; and Doctor Who: *Shroud of
Sorrow*. His non-fiction books for children and their
parents, *Boredom Busters* and *Quick Fixes for Bored
Kids*, have helped him to become a regular guest
on radio stations around the UK and he also writes
for a number of magazines, including *Creative Steps*
and Scholastic's *Junior Education*.

Tommy lives in Lancashire with his family.
He is a huge fan of all things Doctor Who, plays blues
harmonica and makes a mean balloon poodle.

He sees sleep as a waste of good writing time.

You can find out more about Tommy and his books
at his website: www.tommydonbavand.com

Visit the Fangs website at: www.fangsvampirespy.co.uk

TEST YOUR SECRET-AGENT

Spot the Difference (There are eight to spot.)

SKILLS WITH THESE PUZZLES!

The Tickler Facts

How well do you know this book?
Answer these questions and find out!

1) In which country are Fangs and Puppy when they catch Snores?

2) What name does Puppy use when she's undercover at Caramel Cole's Circus?

3) What creature is Wanda Howe, the sword-swallower?

The Tickler Facts

South Africa; Trudy Haslingden; a fairy.

Answers

UNLOCK THE SECRET MISSION FILES!

Want to gain access to highly classified MPI files?

Decode the word below and enter the answer at

WWW.FANGSVAMPIRESPY.CO.UK/MISSION2

Which Fangs character is this?

OPWUY PRNBP

- -